THE SNOW GLOBE FAMILY

For my two great big boys, Robby and Teddy—J.O.C.

To Susan—S.D.S.

PUFFIN BOOKS
Published by the Penguin Group
Penguin Young Readers Group, 345 Hudson Street, New York, New York 10014, U.S.A.
Penguin Group (Canada), 90 Eglinton Avenue East, Suite 700, Toronto, Ontario, Canada M4P 2Y3 (a division of Pearson Penguin Canada Inc.)
Penguin Books Ltd, 80 Strand, London WC2R 0RL, England
Penguin Ireland, 25 St Stephen's Green, Dublin 2, Ireland (a division of Penguin Books Ltd)
Penguin Group (Australia), 250 Camberwell Road, Camberwell, Victoria 3124, Australia (a division of Pearson Australia Group Pty Ltd)
Penguin Books India Pvt Ltd, 11 Community Centre, Panchsheel Park, New Delhi - 110 017, India
Penguin Group (NZ), 67 Apollo Drive, Rosedale, North Shore 0632, New Zealand (a division of Pearson New Zealand Ltd.)
Penguin Books (South Africa) (Pty) Ltd, 24 Sturdee Avenue, Rosebank, Johannesburg 2196, South Africa

Registered Offices: Penguin Books Ltd, 80 Strand, London WC2R 0RL, England

First published in the United States of America by G. P. Putnam's Sons, a division of Penguin Young Readers Group, 2006
Published by Puffin Books, a division of Penguin Young Readers Group, 2008

1 3 5 7 9 10 8 6 4 2

Text copyright © Jane O'Connor, 2006
Illustrations copyright © S. D. Schindler, 2006
All rights reserved

Design by Cecilia Yung and Marikka Tamura. Text set in Biblon.
The pictures were painted with colored inks and gouache.

THE LIBRARY OF CONGRESS HAS CATALOGED THE G. P. PUTNAM'S SONS EDITION AS FOLLOWS:
O'Connor, Jane.
The snow globe family / by Jane O'Connor ; illustrated by S. D. Schindler.
p. cm.
Summary: Two families, one a tiny one that lives in a snow globe in a larger family's home, anxiously await a big snowstorm.
ISBN: 0-399-24242-2 (hc)
[1. Snowdomes—Fiction. 2. Snow—Fiction. 3. Family—Fiction.] I. Schindler, S. D., ill. II. Title.
PZ7.O222Sno 2006—[E]—dc22—2005028560
Puffin Books ISBN 978-0-14-241242-8
Manufactured in China

THE SNOW GLOBE FAMILY

By JANE O'CONNOR • Illustrated by S. D. SCHINDLER

PUFFIN BOOKS

In a big house high on a hill lives a family—
a mama, a papa, a boy, a girl, and Baby.

On the mantel in the parlor sits a snow globe.
It has been there such a long time, nobody notices
it anymore—nobody except Baby.

"Who would like more tea or crumb cake?"
the mama asks.

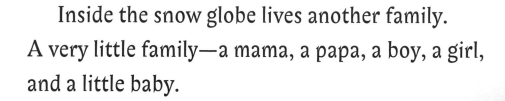

Inside the snow globe lives another family.
A very little family—a mama, a papa, a boy, a girl,
and a little baby.

They are having dessert too, only their cups are so small,
each one holds no more than half a drop of tea.

   "Who would like another crumb of crumb cake?"
the little mama asks.

In the snow globe, sparkly snow
covers the ground all year round.
The little family doesn't mind.
They love snow.

They build snowmen as big as
lumps of sugar.

They skate on a pond
as shiny as a silver coin.

They throw snowballs, make snow angels, and tramp through the snow, leaving footprints smaller than the sprinkles on an ice cream cone.

If only someone in the big family would shake the snow globe really hard and make a hill of snow. Then the little family could go sledding.

Sometimes the little family shouts, "Hellooooo, out there! Look at us!"
But the big papa is reading aloud a story. Nobody notices them—
nobody except Baby.

The little papa is reading a story too. When he's done, the children say, "Tell us about the big snowstorms from long ago. Pleeeease, Papa."

"There used to be snowstorms all the time. Big ones!" their papa begins.

"The house rattled and shook. Dishes flew from the cupboards, furniture slid across the floor.

Once I got thrown out of the bathtub!
Those were the days."

Now there's only a gentle
flurry once a week when the
parlor maid dusts the mantel.

Inside the snow globe, nobody except
the little baby notices. A flurry—who cares?
What the family wants is a great big snowstorm. A blizzard!

That's what the children in the big house are hoping for too.
A blizzard. And one evening, snow starts to fall and doesn't stop.
It is a perfect night for sledding. Off they go, leaving Baby
behind.

"It is your bedtime. The snow will still be here tomorrow," the mama says and goes upstairs to run Baby's bath.

But Baby wants snow now!

Baby pushes her papa's footstool over to the mantel. She piles books and pillows on top. Then up she climbs.

Who does she see inside the snow globe?

She sees the little baby!
What does the little baby see—
two enormous eyes!

Baby grabs the snow globe. Oops! The books and pillows slip from under her. She lands on the pillows and giggles.

She shakes the snow globe. She shakes it some more.

Inside the snow globe, the little family hangs on for dear life.

"Th-th-th-this is s-s-s-some st-storm!"

In the big house, Baby hears her mama calling. "Come, Baby. We'll go sledding too. The snow is too wonderful to miss."

Inside the snow globe, the little family runs outside.
There is a perfect hill for sledding.

WHEEEEEE!

WHEEEEEE!

It is late now. In the big house,
the mama, the papa, and the children
are upstairs, fast asleep.

The snow globe is up on the mantel again.
The little family is fast asleep too.

Everyone—big and little—is dreaming about the next big snowstorm.

Who knows?
It might come very soon.